Good Night,
Little Sea Otter

By Janet Halfmann

Illustrated by Wish Williams

Star Bright Books
Massachusetts

Published in the United States of America by Star Bright Books, Inc.

The name Star Bright Books and the Star Bright Books logo are registered
trademarks of Star Bright Books, Inc.

Please visit www.starbrightbooks.com. For bulk orders, email: orders@starbrightbooks.com, or call
customer service at: (718) 784-9112.

Paperback ISBN-13: 978-1-59572-254-6   Hardback ISBN-13: 978-1-59572-277-5
Star Bright Books / MA / 00208110   Star Bright Books / MA / 00111110
Printed in China / WKT / 10 9 8 7 6 5 4 3 2   Printed in China / WKT / 10 9 8 7 6 5 4 3 2 1

Library of Congress Cataloging-in-Publication Data

Halfmann, Janet.
 Good night, Little Sea Otter / by Janet Halfmann ; illustrations by Wish Williams.
    p. cm.
 Summary: Little Sea Otter tries everything to avoid going to sleep, including saying good night to all
of the creatures above and below the ocean's surface.
 ISBN 978-1-59572-254-6 (pbk. : alk. paper)
 [1. Sea otter--Fiction. 2. Otters--Fiction. 3. Bedtime--Fiction.] I. Williams, Wish, ill. II. Title.
 PZ7.H1386Go 2010
 [E]--dc22
                                2009044869

With lots of love to my grandson, West.
Sweet dreams forever! — J.H.

As the setting sun kissed the kelp forest, Little Sea Otter snuggled on Mama's chest. Mama fluffed her fur until she looked like a brown powder puff.

Then it was bedtime, but Little Sea Otter wasn't ready to sleep. "I forgot to say good night to the harbor seals," she said.

Little Sea Otter waved her soft, silky paw toward the rocky shore.

"Good night, harbor seals," she squealed.

"Good night, Little Sea Otter," they snorted back.

Then loud barks bounced across the waves.

"Oh, I can't forget the sea lions," said Little Sea Otter.

"Good night, father sea lions. Good night, mother sea lions and baby sea lions."

"Sleep tight, Little Sea Otter," barked the sea lions.

A seagull swooped down to check out the commotion. "What's this ruckus about?" squawked the seagull.

"It's bedtime," Mama said.

"Good night, seagull," her little pup called.

"Well, then, Little Sea Otter, good night," squawked the seagull, flying off to find a good resting spot.

"Okay, time to lie down now," said Mama. But before she could say another word, Little Sea Otter dipped her furry face into the chilly water.

"Good night, orange fish and yellow fish and purple fish," she called. "Good night, striped fish and spotted fish. Good night, long fish and short fish."

"Good night, Little Sea Otter," all the fish bubbled and burbled.

"Who else is down there, Mama?" Little Sea Otter asked.

Mama named creature after creature.

"Good night, sea urchins and sea stars. Good night, clams and crabs. Good night, snails and sea slugs," Little Sea Otter called to them all.

"*G-o-o-o-d n-i-i-i-ght,* Little Sea Otter," the entire ocean sang back to her.

Little Sea Otter waited for the *very last* good night. "Did I miss anybody, Mama?"

"Yes, you did," she said, scooping her up in her paws. "You missed ME!"

"Oh! Good night, Mama," she giggled.

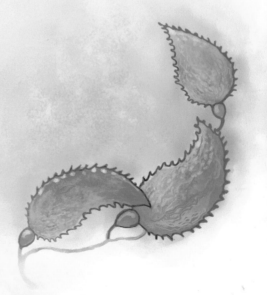

With Little Sea Otter tucked on her chest, Mama rolled over and over in the kelp. Soon they were both wrapped in ribbons of seaweed that would keep them from drifting away during the night.

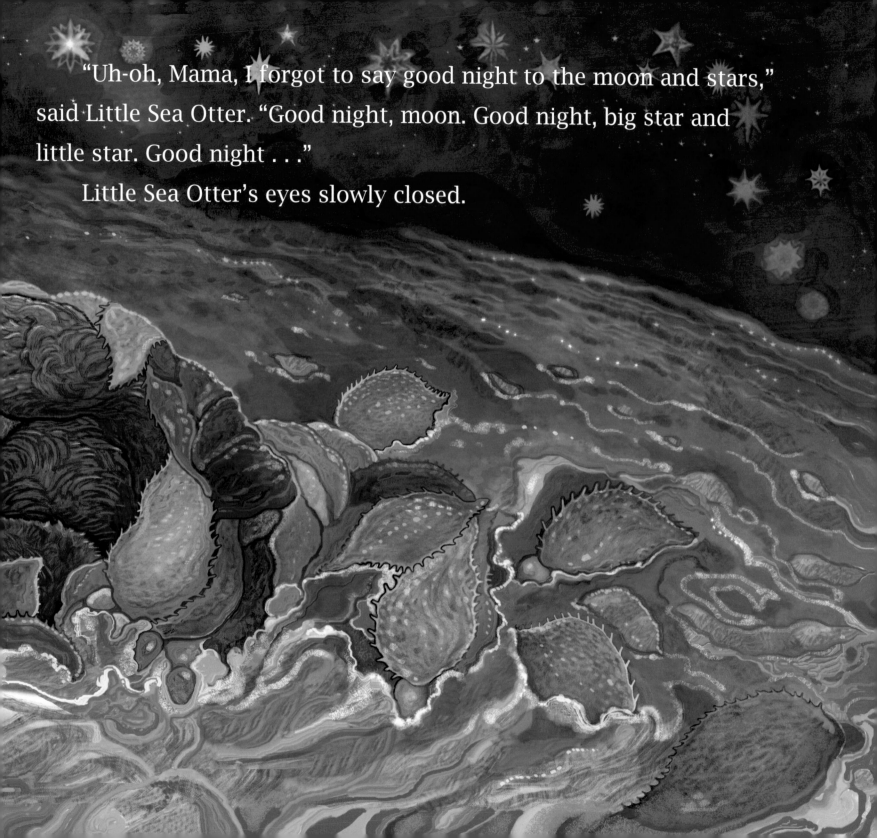

"Uh-oh, Mama, I forgot to say good night to the moon and stars," said Little Sea Otter. "Good night, moon. Good night, big star and little star. Good night . . ."

Little Sea Otter's eyes slowly closed.

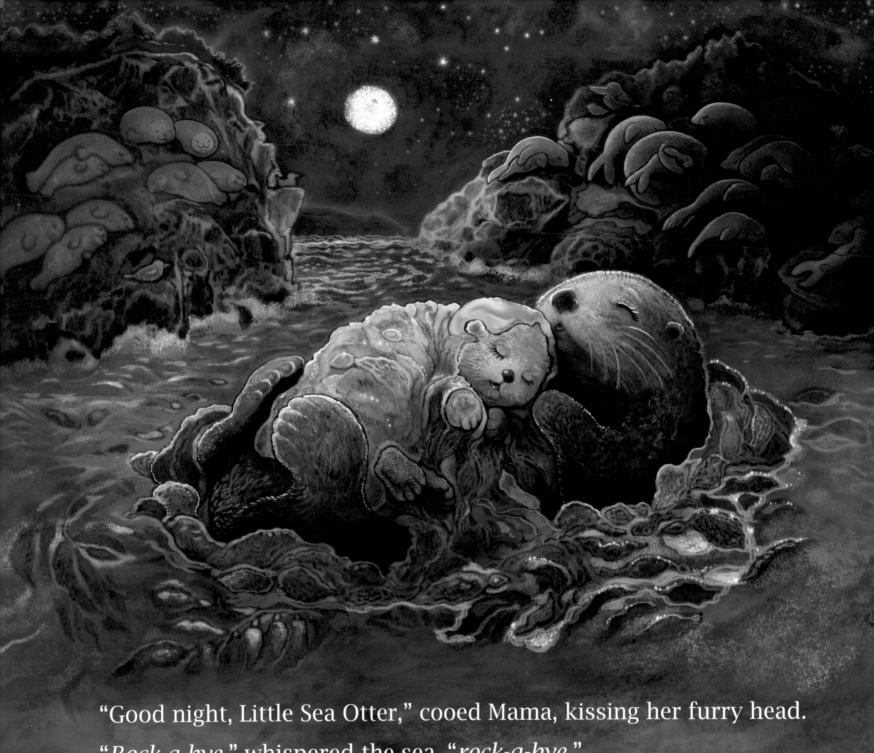

"Good night, Little Sea Otter," cooed Mama, kissing her furry head.

"*Rock-a-bye*," whispered the sea, "*rock-a-bye*."